Emmy
the Exaggerating Elephant

Fenton
the Fearful Frog

Gertie
the Grungy Goat

the Happy Hamster

the Impatient Iguana

Ollie
the Obedient Ostrich

Perry
the Polite Porcupine

Queenie
the Quiet Quail

Rupert
the Resourceful Rhinoceros

Ziggy
the Zippy Zebra

Wendy
the Wise Woodchuck

Xavier
the X-ploring Xenops

Yori
the Yucky Yak

## NOTE TO PARENTS

### Connie, Come Home
### A story about caring

In this story, Connie the Cuddly Cat is feeling lonely, but all her AlphaPet friends are busy and have no time to play with her. Connie thinks that nobody cares for her and decides to run away. When the AlphaPets discover that she's missing, they realize how lonely and sad she was feeling. Can they find her and let her know how much they really care?

In addition to enjoying this adventure with your child, you can use it to teach a gentle lesson about the important value of caring — being sensitive to others' feelings and needs.

You can use this story to introduce the letter **C**. As you read about Connie the Cuddly Cat, ask your youngster to listen for all the **C** words and point to the objects that also begin with **C**. When you've finished reading the story, your child will enjoy doing the activity at the end of the book.

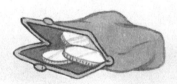

The AlphaPets™ characters were conceived and created by Ruth Lerner Perle.
Characters interpreted and designed by Deborah Colvin Borgo.
Cover design by the Antler & Baldwin Design Group.
Book design and production by Publishers' Graphics, Inc.
Logo design by Deborah Colvin Borgo and Nancy S. Norton.

Printed and Manufactured in the United States of America

# Connie, Come Home

RUTH LERNER PERLE

Illustrated by Deborah Colvin Borgo

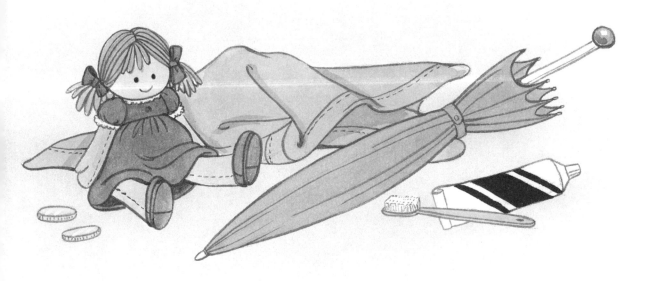

Grolier Enterprises Inc.    Danbury, Connecticut

One day, Connie the Cuddly Cat was looking for something to do.

She picked up a book, but she didn't feel like reading.

She turned on the TV set, but there was nothing she wanted to see.

Then she made a cup of cocoa, but she wasn't thirsty.

And she cut a piece of cake, but she wasn't hungry.

Connie was feeling bored and lonely.

"Maybe another one of the AlphaPets is lonely, too," Connie thought. "Maybe I could find a friend to play with and get some hugs."

Connie loved hugs.

She looked out the window just as Wendy the Wise Woodchuck was walking by.

"Wendy, Wendy!" called Connie. "Would you like some company?"

"Not right now!" answered Wendy. "I'm learning to play the clarinet, and I'm already late for my lesson."

Wendy could tell that Connie was lonely.

"Why don't you go see Gertie the Grungy Goat," she suggested. And she hurried off to music school.

Connie put on her coat and her cap and skipped across
her yard to Gertie's house.

The door was open, but Connie knocked anyway.
"Come right in!" called Gertie.

Connie stepped inside, but when she tried to take another step, she couldn't lift her leg.

*Yuck!* Connie's foot was stuck in a great gooey gob of sticky pink bubble gum! She pulled and pulled and pulled until her foot was finally free.

Connie saw that Gertie was talking on the telephone.

"Gertie, I'm lonely. Can you play with me?" she whispered.

"Maybe this afternoon. I'm on the phone now," said Gertie. "Come back later. And don't trip on my hamburger on your way out!"

So Connie left Gertie's house and went to the park.

There she saw Rupert the Resourceful Rhinoceros. He was skipping from one tree to another, picking things up along the way.

"Oh, Rupert!" Connie shouted. "I'm so happy to see you! Would you like a hug, or someone to dance with?"

"I'm not dancing, you funny cat! I'm collecting chestnuts. Have to pick them up before they're swept away. What a waste! They make beautiful chains, you know. See?"

As Rupert ran to show the chestnuts to Connie, he stumbled and fell.

*Kerplunk!*

The bag broke and the chestnuts came rolling out.

"Oh, no," Rupert groaned. "I'd better get another bag. No time for hugs. No time!" And he dashed out of the park.

Connie was alone again.

It was the same everywhere she went. No one wanted a hug and no one had time for Connie.

Lizzy the Lazy Lamb was taking a nap.

Albert the Absent-minded Alligator was looking for his glasses.

Perry the Polite Porcupine was writing
thank-you notes.

And Yori the Yucky Yak was taking
his spiders for a walk.

Connie decided to try just one more place. She went to the *AlphaPet Super Market*, hoping to meet someone she knew.

Sure enough, there was Delilah the Demanding Duck.

Connie ran over to her. "Hello, Delilah, how about a hug?" she said.

"A hug? A hug?" Delilah cried. "I don't want a hug. I want caramel candy and coconut cookies."

Connie sighed a deep sad sigh and started for home.

By the time Connie got home, she felt very, very sad.

"Nobody loves me. Nobody cares," she sobbed. "I'll run away. That's what I'll do! I'll go to live with my Cousin Cora."

Connie packed her toothbrush, her comb, and her pink blanket with the smooth satin edge all around. She shook all the coins out of her kitty bank and put them in her change purse.

Then she wrote a good-bye note and leaned it against her lamp.

Connie picked up her suitcase, took her favorite doll
and an umbrella, and hurried off to the bus station.

Meanwhile, Wendy's clarinet lesson was over and she thought it would be nice to visit Connie now.

Gertie got off the phone and was ready to play.

Rupert bagged his chestnuts and wondered where Connie had gone.

Delilah was done shopping and now she wanted one of Connie's hugs.

Lizzy woke up from her nap.

Albert found his glasses.

Perry's notes were mailed.

Yori's spiders were tired.

Everybody thought about their dear friend, Connie, and her wonderful, cuddly hugs.

One by one, they all headed for Connie's house.

But Connie's house was empty!

When they read Connie's note, everyone felt terribly  terrible.

"Connie was lonely,  I should have kept her company," said Wendy.

"I should have stopped talking on the phone," cried Gertie.

"I should have danced with her," whispered Rupert.

"Let's try to find Connie and bring her back," said  Perry.

"We have to find her!" demanded Delilah.

Wendy thought for a while. Then she said, "Connie's cousin lives a long way from here. If you ask me, Connie is at the bus station. That is, if the bus hasn't left already!"

They all rushed down to the station together.

And there, waiting at the bus stop, was a very weepy Connie.

"Oh, Connie, please don't leave us," cried the AlphaPets. "We love you and we need your hugs and kisses."

"But I thought no one cared about me," Connie said, brushing away her tears.

Just then, a big green bus arrived. It stopped in front of Connie, and the doors opened.

"All aboard!" called the driver.

Connie picked up her suitcase.

"Don't you dare go!" demanded Delilah.

"Please stay with us," Perry pleaded.

Connie climbed up the bus steps.

"I guess you'd better leave without me," she said to the driver. "I'm going back home with my friends."

"*WHOOPEE!!*" everyone cheered.

"Connie, you *are* a very cuddly cat!"

Here are the words I love the most.
They're really huggable!

cup

coat

carrot

car

calendar

cookies

comb

corn

can

cake

Look back at the pictures in this book and
try to find these and other things that
begin with the letter C.

Aa Bb

Gg Hh

Mm Nn Oo Pp

Uu Vv Ww